Lucy Must Be Traded

 LITTLE SIMON

An imprint of Simon & Schuster Children's Publishing Division

1230 Avenue of the Americas, New York, New York 10020

Manufactured in the United States of America

First Edition 10 9 8 7 6 5 4 3 2 1

ISBN 0-689-86556-2

Adapted from the works of Charles M. Schulz

Lucy Must Be Traded

Adapted by Justine and Ron Fontes
Art adapted by Tom Brannon
Based on the comic strip and characters
created by Charles M. Schulz and the television special
produced by Lee Mendelson and Bill Melendez

LITTLE SIMON
New York   London   Toronto   Sydney

Spring had sprung. The grass was green. The chalk lines on the baseball diamonds had just been drawn. The sky was blue and full of possibilities. It was baseball season! And once again Charlie Brown was faced with the usual bad news.

"Our team is in trouble, Charlie Brown," Linus said. "We're weak at every position!"

"Except right field," Lucy said. "She's exceptionally cute."

Linus ignored his sister. "Our right fielder is completely hopeless," he went on.

"But cute!" Lucy added.

Charlie Brown, the team manager, sighed. His team had never won a game, but somehow he just couldn't give up on his misfit players.

Maybe all Lucy needed was a little more practice. Charlie Brown stepped off the pitcher's mound and yelled to Lucy, "I'm gonna hit you a fly ball."

SMACK! The ball went flying into right field.

Lucy watched it coming toward her. She knew she was supposed to do something. What was it again? Right! She was supposed to catch the ball.

Lucy reached her hand up in time to see the ball whiz past her glove into a bush. Lucy looked through the dense branches. She reached her hand among the twigs but couldn't find the ball. Finally she gave up and carried the whole bush to the pitcher's mound. "It's in here someplace."

"Good grief," Charlie Brown muttered. It was going to be a very long baseball season.

On the night before the first game, Charlie Brown couldn't sleep.
"What kind of manager am I?" he moaned. "I can't run a baseball team.
Nobody listens to me. They all hate me."

The next morning Charlie Brown huddled under the blankets, hoping for rain. "Maybe no one else will show up either," he thought. "I'll just stay in bed and . . ."

Lucy interrupted his thoughts. "Okay, Manager! RISE AND SHINE!" She yelled so loudly that she shouted the blankets right off Charlie Brown.

Charlie Brown's first game of the season was against Peppermint Patty's team. When they got to the field, Peppermint Patty was ready and waiting. "Why don't you warm up, Chuck?" she suggested. "Then we'll start the game."

Charlie Brown agreed, and the players took their positions on the field. "Okay. I'll hit a few flies," he told his teammates. Charlie Brown swung the bat. SMACK! The ball went sailing through the blue sky high over right field. It arced gently toward the green grass—right behind Lucy! This was not a good start.

After she got warmed up, Lucy played even worse! Charlie Brown's team lost the game—and then ten more games after that. When she wasn't making errors, Lucy was busy complaining.

"Well, we lost as usual, Manager," Lucy said after their eleventh defeat. "What are you going to do about it?"

Charlie Brown looked thoughtful. Then he announced, "I've made a big decision. This is the time of year when all the big baseball trades are made. I'm going to try to improve our team with a few shrewd trades."

"That's a great idea," Lucy agreed. "Why don't you trade yourself?"

But Charlie Brown had a different idea.
He called Peppermint Patty.

"Gee, Chuck. The only good player you
have is that little kid with the big nose."

"You mean Snoopy?" Charlie Brown
gasped. "Oh, no. I could never trade him.
I was thinking more of Lucy . . . Hello? Hello?"
Peppermint Patty had hung up!

Later Charlie Brown consulted with Linus. "I told Peppermint Patty I wouldn't ever trade Snoopy, but maybe I was wrong."

Linus was shocked—and so was Snoopy.

"You mean you'd trade your own dog just to win a few games?"

Charlie Brown's eyes glazed over at the word *win*. He wondered what it would be like to be captain of the winning team. He could practically hear the crowd cheer.

Charlie Brown decided to make the trade. Peppermint Patty agreed to give him five players in exchange for Snoopy. But as soon as Charlie Brown hung up the phone, he felt terrible. When he asked Snoopy to forgive him, the beagle turned his back on Charlie Brown.

The rest of the gang had the same reaction.
"Does winning a ball game mean that much to you?" Schroeder demanded.
"I don't know," Charlie Brown said. "I've never won a ball game."
Linus yelled, "I don't even want to talk to you!" Then he snatched away his blanket and added, "And stop breathing on my blanket!"

Charlie Brown couldn't take it anymore. "I was wrong to trade Snoopy. I can see that now," he said, tearing up the contract. "I'm going to tell Peppermint Patty the deal is off!"

Just then Peppermint Patty joined the group and saw the shredded contract. "You must have gotten my message," she said.

"What message?" Charlie Brown asked.

"Those five players I was supposed to trade said they'd quit baseball before they'd play on your team," Peppermint Patty explained. "Sorry, Chuck."

Charlie Brown hid his smile from Peppermint Patty. Snoopy danced with joy.

But that still didn't solve Charlie Brown's problems with Lucy.

"Hey, Manager!" Lucy said. "How come we don't have cleats on our shoes?"

"Cleats?" he asked.

"You know, spikes," Lucy explained. "Whenever I come up to talk to you like this, I wind up sliding down the mound. We'd have a better team if we had cleats on our shoes."

"We'd have a better team if you had something under your cap!" Charlie Brown said.

Lucy shouted back to him from right field, "I bet Babe Ruth had cleats on *her* shoes!"

Charlie Brown couldn't stand it anymore! And Schroeder knew just how he felt. "We've got to get rid of Lucy or we'll never win," Schroeder said.

Just then Lucy told Charlie Brown she was going to stand in the shade because the sun was hurting her eyes. "Why don't you pitch it so they'll hit into the shade?" she suggested.

Suddenly Charlie Brown knew just what to do! "Why don't you play from home from now on?" he said.

"Pour yourself a nice, cold glass of lemonade, sit down in the kitchen, leave the back door open, and I'll pitch the ball so they'll hit it through the door and right to your table," Charlie Brown continued.

Lucy was already home drinking her nice, cold lemonade when it occurred to her that perhaps Charlie Brown was being sarcastic.

So Lucy went back to the field—with a snack.
"What's this?" Charlie Brown asked, pointing to the bench.
"My fielder's glove and a pepperoni pizza for between innings," Lucy explained.
Charlie Brown asked, "What happens if you mix up the glove and the pizza?"

Lucy yelled, "Boy, you must think I'm really stupid!"

But the next fly that came to right field landed in a soft cushion of warm cheese. Sauce splattered all over Charlie Brown's face when he caught Lucy's throw.

Nobody could believe Lucy had actually caught the ball—even with a pizza. She put her glove back on and scrambled onto the right field fence. "Hey, manager! Let's see 'em try to hit one over the fence now."

Sure enough, a high fly came whistling by. SMACK! Lucy caught the ball—and tumbled backward out of the field.

Charlie Brown turned to Schroeder and asked, "Do you think we can get the ball back and leave her on the other side of the fence?"

The next day Peppermint Patty offered to help. "Hey, Chuck. I'm calling to see if you want to trade right fielders."

Charlie Brown was thrilled. "I'd trade Lucy for ANYONE!"

"Marcie isn't a very good player," Peppermint Patty admitted. "But she has a lot of spirit."

In the background, Charlie Brown heard Marcie wailing, "I HATE BASEBALL." But he didn't care. Anyone was better than Lucy!

Even before his first pitch Charlie Brown wondered if he had gotten the better end of the deal. "Marcie, you should be out in right field," he told his new player.

"I'm happier near you, Charles," Marcie said. "Actually, I'm only playing on your team because I've always been fond of you."

"But what if someone hits a ball to right field?" Charlie Brown asked.

Marcie gazed up at him dreamily. "Who cares?"

Meanwhile Peppermint Patty had her hands full with her new right fielder.
"This next hitter is pretty good," she said. "So keep your eye on the ball, Lucille."
Lucy complained, "That's hard to do when you keep moving it around."
Lucy's eyes may have been on the ball, but her glove was nowhere near it!
Peppermint Patty winced as hit after hit bounced on the grass behind Lucy's head.

After the game Peppermint Patty called Charlie Brown. "I made a mistake, Chuck. Lucy's the worst player I've ever seen! You've got to take her back."

Marcie was sad when she heard the trade was over. "I guess I wasn't much help. I didn't score a single goal. I never even made a free throw."

Charlie Brown didn't bother telling her that goals were in soccer and free throws were in basketball. She was Peppermint Patty's problem now.

With his team back together, Charlie Brown took the mound. As he wound up for the pitch he thought, *Maybe now that Lucy's back she'll play better.*

SMACK! The bat smacked the ball into right field. THUMP! The ball bounced off Lucy's umbrella and plopped on the grass.

"Good grief!" Charlie Brown wailed. "It's not even raining."

Lucy laughed. "That's what you think."

THUMP!

KA-BOOM! Thunder boomed, lightning crashed, and rain soaked the field. The team ran for cover, leaving Charlie Brown on the muddy mound. Rain drenched his cap and blurred his vision.

"Hey! Where's everybody going?" Charlie Brown shouted. "It's just a little rain."

As the field filled like a fish pond, Charlie Brown smiled. Another baseball season was over, and he still hadn't won a game. But at least his team was together and . . . there would always be next year.